Baggage

A COMEDY

by

Sam Bobrick

SAMUEL FRENCH

FOUNDED 1830

NEW YORK HOLLYWOOD LONDON TORONTO

SAMUELFRENCH.COM

ISBN 978-0-573-66258-4   Printed in U.S.A.   #4769

IMPORTANT BILLING AND CREDIT
REQUIREMENTS

All producers of *BAGGAGE must* give credit to the Author of the Play in all programs distributed in connection with performances of the Play, and in all instances in which the title of the Play appears for the purposes of advertising, publicizing or otherwise exploiting the Play and/or a production. The name of the Author *must* appear on a separate line on which no other name appears, immediately following the title and *must* appear in size of type not less than fifty percent of the size of the title type.

THE CAST

PHYLLIS NOVAK – A woman in her mid-thirties
BRADLEY NAUGHTON – A man in his late thirties
DR. JONATHAN ALEXANDER – A therapist in his forties
MITZI CARTRIGHT – A woman in her mid to late thirties

ACT I

TIME: *The present. An early spring evening.*

PLACE: *The tastefully furnished, yet uncluttered living room of Phyllis Novak's New York apartment. It is a three story walk up. The front door is at Stage Right. At Stage Left is the entrance to the kitchen. Just below that is a door that leads to the bedroom. A large window is against the Upstage Center wall, flanked by two book-cases. At Center Stage is a sofa, two side chairs, two end tables and a coffee table. A console table is in back of the sofa. At Upstage Right is an attractive desk and chair. A waste basket is next to it. Several lamps and pictures placed throughout, give the apartment a very warm look. Lying on top of the coffee table is a small suitcase lock, a screw driver and a purse.*

AT RISE: **PHYLLIS NOVAK**, *a woman in her mid-thirties, dressed in slacks and a sweater ENTERS from the bedroom pulling a suitcase by its telescopic handle to the center of the room. She pushes the handle back into the suitcase. She then looks about the room and gives it a last minute straightening. The DOORBELL RINGS followed by impatient knocking. Phyllis crosses to the door and opens it.* **BRADLEY NAUGHTON**, *a man in his late thirties, wearing a grey jacket, grey shirt and grey slacks and somewhat out of breath and annoyed stands there.*

BRADLEY. Phyllis Novak?

PHYLLIS. That's me.

(*Using the regular handle, Bradley ENTERS dragging in an identical suitcase. Apparently it is much heavier than the suitcase Phyllis brought out from her bedroom. He stops and tries to catch his breath. Phyllis closes the door*)

7

BRADLEY. Jeez! You didn't tell me there was no elevator in the building.

PHYLLIS. It's only the third floor. I didn't think it would be an issue.

BRADLEY. It wouldn't have been if your damn suitcase wasn't so heavy. What the hell's in here, bricks?

PHYLLIS. *(A bit guilty)* Well, actually there was this little stationary store in Beverly Hills that was going out of business and they had a great deal on paperweights so I bought a few to give out at Christmas.

BRADLEY. How few is a few?

PHYLLIS. Thirty. I have a long gift list.

BRADLEY. Thirty paperweights. It's a wonder the plane was able to take off.

PHYLLIS. It was a little bit much, but I'm the kind of person who upon seeing a good opportunity, takes it.

BRADLEY. I guess I should consider myself lucky they didn't have any file cabinets on sale.

(He has caught his breath and indicates her suitcase)

Where do you want it?

PHYLLIS. Just anywhere.

(Indicates bedroom door)

Over by the bedroom door would be okay.

(Bradley begins to drag the suitcase towards the bedroom)

PHYLLIS, *(continued)* It would probably be easier if you raised up the telescopic handle and wheeled it.

BRADLEY. I would, except it's broken.

PHYLLIS. Oh, no. How did that happen? It's a fairly new bag and it seemed fine when I used it this morning.

BRADLEY. *(Annoyed, he stops dragging the bag and turns to her)* You're not insinuating that I broke it?

PHYLLIS. No. No. Don't be silly. Why would you want to do a thing like that?

BRADLEY. Is that a question?

PHYLLIS. No. Of course not. Still, it does seem curious…

BRADLEY. Let's just end it here, okay?

PHYLLIS. Okay.

BRADLEY. Good.

(He continues to drag the bag to the bedroom door)

I don't get it. Didn't my suitcase, being so much lighter than yours, give you a clue that maybe you were taking the wrong suitcase?

PHYLLIS. If it did, obviously I never would have left with it. When I saw the bag with my initials on it, P.N., I just assumed it was mine and that was that.

BRADLEY. First of all, it didn't have your initials on it. It had mine. B.N. B.N. as in Bradley Naughton and not P.N. as in Phyllis Novak. I admit the bottom part of the "B" was scrapped off a little due to some wear and tear, but if you had looked closely you would have noticed that you could still almost make out that it originally was a "B" not a "P".

(He has finished dragging the bag to the bedroom door)

PHYLLIS. Look, Bradley, I'm sorry you're irritated about our ending up with each others bag and that you've been somewhat inconvenienced but it all worked out. Let's be grateful for that. Besides, I'm sure if you had gone to the baggage claim office and told them what the problem was they would have handled everything. They do that. They would have delivered mine to me and taken yours and delivered it to you and your coming here would have been unnecessary.

BRADLEY. *(Patiently, with a snide attitude)* That sounds all well and good but frankly a bit naive. I know how the airlines operate. If I had gone to the baggage claim office to let them handle this, three things would have happened for certain. You would never see your bag again and I would never see my bag again and someone in Madagascar would have been stuck with thirty paperweights. Fortunately your I.D. tag included your address and phone number and when I saw that you only live four blocks away from me, taking it to my place and calling you made the most sense. Do you mind if I sit down for a minute? I walked from my place with that bag.

(He sits)

PHYLLIS. Oh, that's too bad. You should have taken a cab. I would have gladly shared the expense with you.

BRADLEY. It wasn't the expense. If I got in a cab and told the driver I was only going four blocks, he would have gotten pissed off. I was already pissed off and frankly the last thing I needed was to be in a cab with two pissed off people. Besides, just the thought of lifting the damn bag into a cab again almost gave me a hernia. Is there a chance you might offer me a cold drink or something?

PHYLLIS. Oh, certainly.

(She stands there for a moment, trying to get herself together, obviously overwhelmed by Bradley's annoyance)

BRADLEY. Well, okay. Offer it.

PHYLLIS. Would you like a cold drink or something?

BRADLEY. That would be nice. That's very thoughtful.

PHYLLIS. God, you are a handful, aren't you?

(Phyllis EXITS to kitchen)

BRADLEY. I'm an attorney with the IRS. I need to be. Maybe next time you travel you should tie a little red ribbon on your handle to help you identify your bag. That way screw-ups like this won't happen.

PHYLLIS *(ENTERS with a can of soda)* Well, by the same token, you could have put a little red ribbon on your bag.

BRADLEY. Forget it. Men don't do that. That's a woman thing.

PHYLLIS. Well, then maybe you should tie a man thing around your handle.

BRADLEY. Like what?

PHYLLIS. How about an athletic supporter? That seems somewhat masculine. I could go one step further but that could be too picturesque. How's a diet root beer?

BRADLEY. Fine. Thanks.

PHYLLIS. Do you want a glass?

BRADLEY. Did you bring one?

PHYLLIS. No.

BRADLEY. Then you obviously think I don't need one.

(*Opens the can and takes a swallow*)

Jeez, it's been just one of those stupid days. From the time I left L.A. it's been one screw up after another. I had trouble checking out of the hotel. I almost missed the damn airplane. I sat next to a woman with a screaming kid. And the stupid lunch they served us. I think it was supposed to be pot roast. I was nauseous from the first bite. I really don't think meat should be blue. Why I ate it, I'll never know. Goddamn airlines. Unless they screw up your day they're not happy.

PHYLLIS. Well, they got us here safe and sound and basically nowadays that's all you can hope for.

BRADLEY. Please, don't try to make me feel better. I'm not in the mood for it.

PHYLLIS. Look, it's obvious you're upset so I will take full responsibility for the luggage mix-up and apologize profusely and after you finish your drink you can take your suitcase and be on your way. How's that?

BRADLEY. I wouldn't be surprised if that made us both very happy.

PHYLLIS. I have a strong suspicion it will.

(*Notices the little lock on the lamp table*)

Oh, darn. I forgot to put your lock back on.

BRADLEY. What lock?

PHYLLIS. This little lock that was on your suitcase.

(*Gets the lock and hands it to him*)

BRADLEY. You unlocked my suitcase?

PHYLLIS. It wasn't difficult. Those little locks are really a joke. A kitchen knife or a tiny screw driver opens all of them.

BRADLEY. *(Annoyed)* That's not the point. You opened my suitcase. You didn't need to open my suitcase? Everything you needed to know was on the outside I.D. tag. Name, address, phone number…What was the need to open my suitcase? That's a total violation of my privacy. I didn't open yours.

PHYLLIS. Well, you were coming to my apartment. This is New York. You don't just let anyone come to your apartment in New York. I wanted to know a little bit about you just in case I thought I might need to have a cop here.

BRADLEY. You should have gotten one. Maybe he could have helped me carry your goddamn suitcase up the stairs.

PHYLLIS. Anyway, after looking through your photo album I really didn't think I needed to bring anyone else into this. Your eyes seemed to indicate there was a reasonable touch of sanity behind them which proves pictures can be misleading.

BRADLEY. You looked through my photo album? Those were my wedding pictures.

PHYLLIS. I know. It said so on the imitation leather cover. "The wedding of Joyce and Bradley." Joyce is quite pretty.

BRADLEY. Yes, she is. Damn it, you really had no business…

PHYLLIS. And she seemed so radiantly happy.

BRADLEY. She was. We both were. Look, I really think you owe me a…

PHYLLIS. It's such a pity it didn't work out.

BRADLEY. Oh, no. You read the letters. You read my letters. How dare you…

PHYLLIS. Look, don't give yourself a seizure. Yes, I did read them and I'm sorry. And I know I shouldn't have. I happen to be a very inquisitive person.

BRADLEY. Nosey, is more like it.

PHYLLIS. Yes. Maybe that too. I guess it goes with the territory.

BRADLEY. I think the territory is breaking and entering. God, what a snoop you are. Maybe you should get a job with the CIA. They could use your kind of help.

PHYLLIS. Oh, get off it. I'm an editor at Putnam. I read books all day long and over the years, I developed this acute curiosity problem. I now have this overwhelming need to know how things end. It's a stupid and annoying hang up and I desperately wish I could get over it but I can't and most likely won't. When I started going through your album, I found the pictures of you and Joyce absolutely mesmerizing.

BRADLEY. *(Suddenly interested)* You did?

PHYLLIS. I did. You see, there seemed to be such an overwhelming certainty in both your faces that your marriage was going to last forever no matter what.

BRADLEY. Yes. Yes, we did have that look, didn't we?

PHYLLIS. Yes, you did. The photographer must have really done some heavy duty touching up.

BRADLEY. He did do some, but honestly, not that much.

PHYLLIS. And then those letters, they were tied together so nicely, so sweetly, with that cute little frilly red ribbon...

BRADLEY. *(Embarrassed)* I swear, that's the only time I've used a red ribbon.

PHYLLIS. That's not the point. It was obviously tied with care and affection. And I was truly happy for you. I thought, God, maybe they know the secret.

BRADLEY. The secret to what?

PHYLLIS. To a happy, trusting, lasting relationship. In this day and age relationships of that nature are not easy to come by. I should know. I've been through a few of them.

BRADLEY. I'm not surprised. Who wants to live their life with a spy?

PHYLLIS. For your information, Bradley, all the breakups were my doing.

BRADLEY. Well, that's what you say.

PHYLLIS. No, it's true. It's very true. I'm just too cautious. I want a hundred percent guarantee that my choice is going to be the right one, the perfect one. And as the relationship progresses I always seem to find a flaw that starts out small, but one that I soon find so overwhelming I know I'll never be able to live with it. It could be anything, the way he eats, the sounds he makes when he sleeps, the TV shows he likes…I seem to be hung up on finding the perfect mate which I know doesn't exist, yet I can't seem to make myself settle for anything less.

BRADLEY. You're obviously a bit of a nut case.

PHYLLIS. That's possible.

BRADLEY. I honestly don't know why you're telling me all this. Frankly, I couldn't care less. I didn't come up here to make a friend.

PHYLLIS. And believe me, you haven't. Maybe that's the reason I'm being so open about my situation. I think I need to hear myself admit the fact that I have a problem. Since we don't really know one another and most likely won't see each other again, I'm probably more comfortable opening up to you than I would be to a closer and more sympathetic acquaintance. I know I definitely have a commitment problem and it's obviously bothering me. When I finally agree to "till death do us part" I want to be sure I have a shot at it.

BRADLEY. How the hell does anyone know how anything's going to end up? Especially marriage. I certainly didn't. And as for the perfect husband, I thought I was one. Five days a week I left the house early in the morning and I didn't come back until late at night. Except for weekends Joyce hardly saw me. What more can a wife ask for?

(He opens up his suitcase and starts checking through it)

PHYLLIS. What are you doing?

BRADLEY. I'm just checking to see that everything that's supposed to be here still is.

PHYLLIS. Oh, please, you don't think I would…

BRADLEY. I don't know what I think.

PHYLLIS. Well, I didn't take anything. By the way, your taste in clothes is a little on the sorrowful side. Almost everything is grey. You're not an old man. Brighten up. Try a little color. It may just add a drop of cheer to your personality.

BRADLEY. Forget it. In my frame of mind, the only other color that makes sense is black.

(He pulls out the stack of various size envelopes tied with a red ribbon and begins counting them)

One, two, three, four…

PHYLLIS. Trust me, your letters are all there. All eleven of them.

BRADLEY. There were twelve of them.

PHYLLIS. Well, you can't really count the cease and desist from her lawyer.

(Bradley leers at her and puts the envelopes back)

Tell me. Why do you keep those letters of hers? They aren't very nice.

BRADLEY. How about it's none of your business?

PHYLLIS. God, she accused you of everything. I don't remember every accusation but the words, boring, humorless, indifferent and cranky sort of stick out. After reading her letters, if all she said about you is true, I can understand her wanting out of the marriage.

BRADLEY. Maybe it's possible I could be boring and humorless and cranky, but believe me, not that it's any of your concern, the last thing I am is indifferent. I wish I was. Maybe, I wouldn't be taking this break-up so hard. You want to know the real reason she left me? It's very simple. We went to her high school class reunion. Her high school sweetheart showed up and she ran off to California with him. That usually will put a damper on any marriage. Now let's just drop the subject, okay.

PHYLLIS. Okay. *(A beat)* How was your sex life?

BRADLEY. You know, I don't really think that's any of your business either.

PHYLLIS. Of course it isn't. But let me offer this to you. The majority of the books my company publishes are what we refer to as kitchen novels, novels written mostly by housewives. In ninety-five percent of them, the first thing to go wrong in a marriage is the sex life.

BRADLEY. Maybe if those housewives spent more time taking care of their husband instead of writing those stupid books you wouldn't have those statistics. Besides, for your information, our sex life was damn good. Once, twice, quite often three times a month. With all the pressures we have to endure that's almost remarkable for a New Yorker.

PHYLLIS. I guess so.

BRADLEY. Besides, we were married almost four years. You can't keep a marriage hot and heavy forever you know. I didn't have a clue she wasn't happy. Wherever we'd go, we'd always hold hands. Except of course at her high school class reunion. Why did I ever agree to attend? She danced almost every dance with that stupid ex-boyfriend of hers.

PHYLLIS. And where were you?

BRADLEY. At the shrimp bar. I like shrimp. It was all you can eat for ten bucks. They lost a bundle on me. I was there for hours. Since she left me I haven't been able to even look at a shrimp. I don't know why I'm even talking to you about it. I feel lousier now then when I came up here. I need to go.

(Shuts the suitcase and puts the lock on it)

Let me warn you now, If I'm missing anything I'll make sure you get a tax audit.

PHYLLIS. You went to L.A. to obviously try to talk her into coming back to you, didn't you?

BRADLEY. I don't know why I went to L.A. What does it matter? All I did for six days was stay in my hotel room. I didn't make any calls. I didn't go out. I didn't do anything. I ate all my meals in my rooms. I think the airlines and the hotel had the same chef. I don't know if you can understand this, but I just wanted to be in the same city with her. It was crazy and I was crazy and now here I am talking to you and I think you're crazy.

(He sits on the sofa and buries his head in his hands)

Damn it, I really miss her. I really, really, really miss her.

PHYLLIS. *(An awkward moment. She doesn't know what to say)* You really miss her, don't you?

BRADLEY. *(Looks up)* Didn't I just say that? I thought I just said that.

(He begins to weep and sniffle)

PHYLLIS. Yes, yes, you did.

(Bradley continues to weep)

Are you crying?

BRADLEY. Yes, I'm crying.

PHYLLIS. Oh, my.

BRADLEY. I miss her so much. So very, very much.

PHYLLIS. I know. I know. Gosh, I hate sending you home this way. Would you like a paperweight?

(He gives her a stare)

I'm sorry. I don't know why I said that.

(Bradley continues to weep throughout)

I have to admit, I'm really impressed by a man's crying.

BRADLEY. I'm thrilled to hear that.

PHYLLIS. No, really. Not that I like it but it's actually very moving. It shows sensitivity. I would never have guessed that about you. None of the men I was serious about ever cried.

BRADLEY. Maybe had you married any of them, they would have. Do you have any Kleenex?

PHYLLIS. Yes, of course.

(She hands him a box. He takes out one and begins blowing his nose)

BRADLEY. *(He has control of himself now)* Maybe we should have had children. That might have kept her home. Men seldom run off with women who have children.

PHYLLIS. Why didn't you have any?

BRADLEY. She wouldn't stop taking her birth control pills. My life is a mess.

PHYLLIS. I know.

BRADLEY. I can't ever see it getting any better.

PHYLLIS. Most likely it won't.

BRADLEY. *(Annoyed)* Why are you agreeing with me?

PHYLLIS. I'm sorry. I just didn't think right now was a good time not to.

BRADLEY. *(Begins weeping again)* I miss my wife.

PHYLLIS. I know.

BRADLEY. Why? Why did she leave me?

PHYLLIS. Boring, humorless, indifferent, cranky and an ex-boyfriend.

BRADLEY. *(Stops weeping)* God, you are a big help, aren't you? I should go home. I hate losing control like this.

PHYLLIS. I know. It's not a pretty picture.

BRADLEY. I thought you said you liked it when men cry?

PHYLLIS. I do, but it's still not a pretty picture.

BRADLEY. *(Takes a deep breath. Composed)* I think I'm okay, now.

PHYLLIS. Good.

BRADLEY. I'll be on my way. It was fairly nice meeting you.

PHYLLIS. Same here.

BRADLEY. *(About to get up, he falls back on the sofa and begins weeping again)* Why? Why did she go?

PHYLLIS. God, I feel so badly for you.

BRADLEY. Me too.

PHYLLIS. Look, do you have any plans for dinner?

BRADLEY. Yes. I was going to go home and take some poison.

(He stops his crying and is now just sniffling a bit)

PHYLLIS. Okay, here's an offer. I know you're not in a good place and I feel some of it is my fault. This suitcase incident seems to have pushed you over the edge. Anyway, at this particular time, I don't think it's a wise thing for you to be alone. Now, I haven't eaten since the airplane and you probably haven't either, so what if we had dinner together tonight?

BRADLEY. I hope you're not planning to try and cheer me up?

PHYLLIS. No. That may not be possible. I just thought that maybe you might need to be with someone until you can pull yourself together.

BRADLEY. *(He has his crying under control)* Oh, really? Well, quite frankly you would be the last person I'd want to be with, Miss Snoop.

PHYLLIS. No. I think quite frankly I would be the best person you could be with. I already know your story so you won't have to go through it again. We can talk about other things just to get your mind off of Joyce. Movies, books. It won't have to be a long dinner. I have to be at work in the morning and I assume you do too. And, since you brought my bag over, I insist on picking up the check.

BRADLEY. You're offering to buy me dinner?

PHYLLIS. I am.

BRADLEY. That's really very decent of you and very unexpected. I might like that. I might like that very much. For once in my life I might come out on top.

PHYLLIS. Good. Besides shrimp, what other kinds of food do you like? How about French?

BRADLEY. How about Italian?

PHYLLIS. I don't think Italian's good for you. You apparently get acid build up.

BRADLEY. Oh, no. You looked through my toiletries? You found my Tums. Why did you look through my toiletries?

PHYLLIS. Well, I wanted to see if you took any anti-depressants. After what you've been through you may want to consult your doctor about getting some. They're quite wonderful.

BRADLEY. Do you take them?

PHYLLIS. Do you think I could have gotten through this encounter with you if I didn't? Come on. Let's leave right now before you start crying again.

(She grabs her purse off the table, takes Bradley by the arm and leads him to the door)

BRADLEY. I'm not sure this is a good idea.

PHYLLIS. *(Opening the door)* It probably isn't but we can talk about that at dinner. Oh another thing. Your bottle of Advil has expired.

BRADLEY. Oh, jeez.

(She pushes him out the door, turns off the light switch on the wall and follows him out, closing the door behind them)

BLACKOUT

End Act I, Scene 1

Scene 2

The stage is dark. **DR. JONATHAN ALEXANDER**, *a therapist in his 40's, walks out from the wings to the footlights
Center Stage. A spot follows him.*

JONATHAN. How do you do. I'm Doctor Jonathan Alexander, a professional, licensed psychologist with degrees
from several prestigious Universities, a B.A., an M.A.,
a P.H.D, etcetera, etcetera. I deal mainly in couples
counseling and have written a number of books on
the subject, among them COUPLES IN CONFLICT,
COUPLES IN COMBAT, and the recently published
COUPLES IN HELL. All of them about nipping bad
relationships in the bud. What you are watching, obviously, is a story about two people who are absolutely
so wrong for each other, but never-the-less become
involved with each other and most likely at the end of
the play end up together. A wonderful, neat little story,
that we seem to encounter in movies and plays over
and over and over again. Frankly, for my taste, I find
these sort of stories a bit trite, but that's not important.
What is important is that they are really very misleading and does you, the audience, a great disservice.
Ladies and gentlemen, in my professional and knowl-
edgeable opinion, you are watching a train wreck
about to happen. I don't care how the play ends, this
is a relationship that won't and can't work and unfor-
tunately two years down the line I'm afraid they're
going to find that out. I know what I'm talking about.
I've been down this road several times myself with the
wrong partner. That's why I got into this line of work
in the first place. Phyllis and Bradley are two very, very
troubled people who, if they had any common sense,
would get out of each others lives as fast as they can.
Let's start with Bradley. Bradley! Just his name makes
me shudder. It really says it all, doesn't it? Angry, confused and whinny. God, I just hate to see a man cry.
Certainly, there are times when it can't be helped,

like over the loss of a loved one or when your favorite baseball team loses the World Series, but for the most part it shows a definite lack of confidence and control, not really a desirable attribute in a man. And as for Phyllis, I, myself, would rather get run over by a semi-truck than get involved with someone like her. I've seen controlling women before but she takes the cake. Strong, domineering, opinionated, she would rather live anyone else's life but her own. What the hell can these two very troubled and contradictory people expect from this sort of union? What happens after they marry and are up to their necks in kids and house payments and car payments and school tuitions and insurance payments and realize they are both now living a life of unfulfillment, unhappiness and ulcers? The point I'm making is that life is not a play. You've got to think past the happy ending for crying-out-loud. If two people aren't right for each other at the beginning of the relationship, they haven't got a prayer in hell of working it out down the line. I'll have more to say about this as the evening progresses. Anyway, Phyllis and Bradley have eaten and they're on their way back to her place, so I'd better get going. Oh, by the way, at the end of the play, you'll have an opportunity to buy all three of my books in the lobby. Thank you.

(The LIGHTS FADE TO BLACK as he walks off)

End Act I, Scene 2

Scene 3

TIME: Later that evening.

The apartment is dark. We hear a key in the lock. The door opens and Phyllis ENTERS and turns on the light. She is followed by Bradley who goes right to his suitcase, lifts the telescopic handle and starts to wheel it towards the door.

BRADLEY. *(Annoyed)* Well, goodbye and good luck. It's been an experience.

PHYLLIS. The very least you can do is say thanks.

BRADLEY. No. The very least I can do is get the hell out of here and never see you again. How could you do what you did?

PHYLLIS. What did I do?

BRADLEY. It could have been a tolerable evening, maybe even a nice evening, but no, you had to ruin it by inviting that obnoxious woman to our table. And then to tell her everything about what I'm going through. How callous are you?

PHYLLIS. Mitzi Cartright is one of my very dearest friends. I had no idea she was going to be at the restaurant and since she was by herself I thought it was only polite to ask her to join us. And I had no idea you were so concerned about keeping your situation a secret, especially after you were so open about it with both the waiter and maitre 'de.

BRADLEY. Well, when they saw me crying, I had to tell them something. What if they blamed it on the food or the service? Why should they go home feeling upset?

PHYLLIS. Look, I thought Mitzi was someone you might like to get to know. Especially since you both seem to be in similar situations. You had a bad marriage, she had a bad marriage.

BRADLEY. Correction. She had three bad marriages.

PHYLLIS. Regardless. I had optimistically hoped you might find comfort in each other's misfortune. So I was wrong. I'm sorry.

BRADLEY. First of all, let me correct you on one other little thing. I did not have a bad marriage. I had a great marriage. It was my wife that seemed to have the bad marriage. Besides, how could you possibly think someone like Mitzi could ever comfort me. So loud, so pushy, the way she insisted we all taste each other's food.

PHYLLIS. That's what people do in a Chinese restaurant.

BRADLEY. Yeah, well, I don't. When I order in a restaurant, I order something I want to eat, not the crap everybody else orders. She took a bite, you took a bite, the people at the next table took a bite, when my plate finally came back to me the only thing left on it were three hot peppers and a fish bone from someone else's meal. That's why people are always hungry two hours after leaving a Chinese restaurant.

PHYLLIS. I'm afraid your ex-wife was right. You are very cranky.

BRADLEY. No, I'm very hungry. That's what makes me cranky. Do you have any milk?

PHYLLIS. Low fat milk.

BRADLEY. May I have a glass. My stomach is killing me. I shouldn't have eaten those three hot peppers.

PHYLLIS. I'll get the milk.

(She EXITS to kitchen)

BRADLEY. Thank you. My stomach is actually making hunger noises. As soon as I get home I'm making a peanut butter and jelly sandwich for myself and eating it in a closet where I can be sure I won't have to share it with anybody. And another thing. I hated the fortune in my stupid fortune cookie. Everyone had a nice one but me. "Stay away from chocolate." What kind of dopey fortune is that? I love chocolate. It's the only decent thing left in my life.

PHYLLIS. *(ENTERS with a glass of milk.)* I'm sorry. I couldn't hear what you were saying.

(She hands him the milk)

BRADLEY. It doesn't matter. Repeating it would just give one of us a headache.

(He takes a sip of milk)

You know what really irks me?

PHYLLIS. I would say about ninety-five percent of everything in the world.

BRADLEY. That you could even think that someone like Mitzi could ever appeal to me.

PHYLLIS. Look, I'm not in the matrimony business. It just seemed you two had a lot in common. She's pathetic, you're pathetic, I thought it was a perfect match.

BRADLEY. Maybe in hell it would be, but at Uncle Wong Fu's Chinese Grill, it wasn't. There was absolutely no chemistry between us. Not a bit.

PHYLLIS. Really. Then why did you give her your phone number?

BRADLEY. She asked me for it. She was a friend of yours and I didn't want to be rude. Besides, I'm changing my number anyway. All I seem to get are calls from people who want to sell me something. Every time I explain what happened to my marriage, they all seem to side with my ex-wife, those that don't hang up.

PHYLLIS. Well, Mitzi sided with you. She was the only one in the entire restaurant who did.

BRADLEY. That's not so. Jose, the waiter, seemed very sympathetic.

PHYLLIS. Trust me. He wasn't. He just wanted a good tip.

BRADLEY. I hope you left him one.

PHYLLIS. I did. Anyway, I think except for the two or three times you got into a crying jag again, it wasn't that bad an evening. Between you and me, I think if Mitzi calls you, you should give her a chance.

BRADLEY. Forget it. She's been married three times and dumped three times. There's a message there and I believe I got it.

(Starts to cry again)

What am I going to do without Joyce? I'll die without her, I know I will.

PHYLLIS. Don't. Please don't cry anymore. It's starting to become annoying.

BRADLEY. I can't help myself. I miss her so much. Her soft velvet hair, her cute little button nose, those beautiful blue eyes of hers…or were they brown? They may have been brown. I'm not sure. I never actually looked that closely. Oh, God, I miss that woman.

PHYLLIS. Weren't you ever a little bit suspicious your marriage was in trouble?

BRADLEY. Not for a minute. I thought she was happy, I thought I was happy. You can't ask for better than that. Believe me, I would have done anything to make the marriage work. I loved married life. In the winter, when we went to bed there was always someone I could warm my cold feet on. In the summer, I always had someone to put sun screen on my back. New Year's Eve I always had a date. I am a man in pain.

PHYLLIS. You want some good advice?

BRADLEY. No. You've been giving me advice all evening. Even at the Chinese restaurant. I ordered the Kung Pao Chicken because you told me to.

PHYLLIS. I thought it was an excellent choice.

BRADLEY. I wouldn't know. I never got a chance to stick a fork in it, remember?

PHYLLIS. Okay, well here's the last bit of advice I'm giving you and you'll be smart to consider it very seriously. The only chance you have of becoming healthy enough to fit back into society again is to get involved with someone else as quickly as you can, even if it's only a superficial relationship. Just someone to help get your mind off of both Joyce and yourself because you're building it into something much bigger than it was and all you're going to do is get more and more depressed and end up in worse shape then you're in now.

BRADLEY. Well, I'm not getting involved with your friend, Mitzi. She is so wrong for me it's not funny. I'd even rather be involved with you than with her.

(More crying)

I'm going to die. I know it. I feel it. I once read an article where a guy wished himself dead and he died. Maybe after tax season I'll give it more thought.

PHYLLIS. All right! All right! I'll do it.

BRADLEY. Do what?

PHYLLIS. What you suggested. I'm going to let you get involved with me.

BRADLEY. Wait a minute. I didn't suggest it. You suggested it.

PHYLLIS. I suggested you get involved with someone. You mentioned me. I just thought it over and it makes good sense.

BRADLEY. What do you mean you thought it over. I just mentioned it two seconds ago.

PHYLLIS. I have a mind that processes things very quickly.

BRADLEY. Look, I was just rambling. I really don't like you that much, if at all.

PHYLLIS. That's not the point. The point is, I think our getting involved with each other is a wonderful idea for both of us. By concentrating on me, there would be less room in your head for your ex-wife. I'll keep you busy. I'll fill up the space she left and then some. We'll go to plays, to movies, we'll go for walks. I'll make you do things that will bring you back into the world again.

BRADLEY. What about bowling?

PHYLLIS. No. I draw the line at bowling.

BRADLEY. Just asking.

PHYLLIS. I'll see that you won't have time to think about Joyce. You'll find I'm a very strong, determined and focused woman which is what you need at this time to make you fit to live among people again.

BRADLEY. *(A beat)* Okay, what's the catch?

PHYLLIS. What do you mean, what's the catch?

BRADLEY. I mean what's in it for you?

PHYLLIS. All right. I'll level with you, but don't take this the wrong way. Being with you for as short a time as I have, I realize that there wasn't one guy that I went with that was half the pain in the ass you are.

BRADLEY. So?

PHYLLIS. You're annoying, you're difficult, you're practically hopeless. You're everything your ex-wife said you were if not more.

BRADLEY. Oh, so now you're taking her side too.

PHYLLIS. No, not at all. Here it is in a nutshell, Bradley. All my life I've been looking for the perfect guy when deep down inside I know there is no such animal. The problem is, I can't get myself to accept that. By forcing myself to be around you for any length of time, I have a feeling that anyone that comes my way after you, is going to look like Prince Charming by comparison. Maybe, after a month or two with you, just maybe, I'll finally be able to compromise, to settle, to be more tolerant of male shortcomings and maybe, just maybe, I won't be doomed to spinsterhood.

BRADLEY. So then you'd be using me.

PHYLLIS. Yes. And you'd be using me.

BRADLEY. That is so sick.

PHYLLIS. Yes. But so are we. In our own way. You, of course, worse than me. You need to be forced to forget about a marriage that is over and I need to be forced to get real about relationships, otherwise we're going to end our days as the stupid sad souls that we are.

BRADLEY. So what we'd be doing is going steady in a superficial sort of way.

PHYLLIS. Yes. A very superficial sort of way.

BRADLEY. For how long?

PHYLLIS. Let's say until one of us is so fed up with the other that they may need to be institutionalized.

BRADLEY. What about sex?

PHYLLIS. Take your pants off and I'll punch your lights out.

BRADLEY. No sex?

PHYLLIS. None.

BRADLEY. That's more like being married than going steady.

PHYLLIS. Just keep in mind, Bradley, this is not a romance. It's a companionship.

BRADLEY. Companionship? Don't you have to be in your eighties for something like that? I don't know. I might need a few days to mull this around, let it simmer in my head a bit.

PHYLLIS. If you're smart you'll give me a "yes" right now. In a few days there's a chance that I may come to my senses.

BRADLEY. Let me think...Let me think. The two of us seeing each other...dating...but not really dating. I really don't like the idea but I have to admit anything's better than this constant wallowing in the pain. Okay...I'll do it. Yes! I say yes! I'll try anything to get over Joyce, to forget her... *(Sadly)*...her soft velvet hair, her cute little button nose, those beautiful...

PHYLLIS. Okay, okay. We already went through that list.

BRADLEY. Maybe if I show you some recent pictures of her you'll know what I'm going through. May I? I have several in my wallet.

PHYLLIS. If you must.

(Bradley takes several pictures from his wallet and hands them to Phyllis)

BRADLEY. Here. I heard she's gotten even more attractive since she left me.

PHYLLIS. *(Taking them and looking at them)* She's very pretty. But from now on, I'm the woman in your life.

(She tears the pictures in half and hands them back to Bradley)

BRADLEY. That was very cruel.

PHYLLIS. I know. But either we go at this one hundred percent or not at all.

BRADLEY. You're tough.

PHYLLIS. You've got that part right.

BRADLEY. Damn it, I hate to admit it but in a crazy way this just might work. I already feel my anger for Joyce slowly turning towards you.

PHYLLIS. Good. Now when do you want to start?

BRADLEY. Why not tomorrow? Monday's are always saddest for me and until football season rolls around in the fall, there's nothing really worth watching on TV.

PHYLLIS. Okay, tomorrow it is. We'll try a movie.

BRADLEY. What about dinner?

PHYLLIS. Something healthy.

BRADLEY. I'd rather have something good.

PHYLLIS. We'll see.

BRADLEY. I can't believe I'm buying into this. It just proves how desperate I am. Still, I have to admit Phyllis, it's so very, very kind of you to do this.

(Starts to snivel)

No one's really ever gone out of their way for me.

PHYLLIS. Don't start crying. Please, don't start crying.

BRADLEY. No more. No more. I promise.

(Controlling himself)

Well, good night, Phyllis. I'll see you tomorrow, let's say about seven.

PHYLLIS. Fine. Good night, Bradley.

BRADLEY. Boy, it's really been some wild day, huh?

(Bradley starts out)

PHYLLIS. Uh, Bradley. Aren't you forgetting something?

BRADLEY. Oh, I'm sorry.

(He goes over and kisses her on the cheek)

Good night, Phyllis.

PHYLLIS. I meant your suitcase.

BRADLEY. Oh, right. Right. Thanks.

(He goes to his bag and wheels it to the door)

See you tomorrow night.

(He EXITS. Phyllis stands at the door for a moment, shakes her head, closes the door and then approaches the audience)

PHYLLIS. Let me explain how I've been thinking. Here I am, a very cautious, unattached, independent, not unattractive, woman, with no guy in sight and not getting any younger. Okay, along comes Bradley Naughton, a guy who is not bad looking, clean, apparently no criminal record, has a good job, is emotionally needy and ripe for the picking with only one slight problem. He's not my type. So here's my plan. It's very simple. I will turn Bradley Naughton into my type. George Bernard Shaw sort of did that in Pygmallion and that worked out fine. It's not going to be that difficult. He's already beaten down so the resistance will be almost nil. I will simply win his confidence, make him very dependent on me and what I don't like about him, I'll change. In no time at all, Bradley Naughton will be the perfect man for me. Trust me, when I finish with him you will like him so much more than you do now. And what about his hang up with his ex-wife? Well, did you listen to him? In all the time he kept crying and moaning about missing her, did you once here the word "love" mentioned? I didn't. That should tell you something. Anyway, I think it's a positive opportunity. Devious? Underhanded? Unethical? Yes. But in today's market, not a bad option for a single girl over thirty. Especially one as…spirited and picky and terrified about relationships as myself. Okay, I know what you're thinking.

What about love on my part? Well, I've been living without it so far and as you can see, it hasn't affected me in the least. But it's time for me to settle down and I do believe Bradley and I can have a very nice life together. I promise you, it's going to work out fine. I'll have to write the airlines a thank you note.

(Jonathan ENTERS from the wings.)

JONATHAN. Excuse me! Excuse me.

PHYLLIS. *(Confused)* Yes?

JONATHAN. How do you do. I'm Doctor Jonathan Alexander. I'm a professional, licensed psychologist with degrees from many prestigious Universities, a B.A., an M.A., a PHD, etcetera, etcetera. The audience already met me. I deal mainly in couples counseling and have written a number of books on the subject.

PHYLLIS. And what seems to be the problem?

JONATHAN. I need to warn you Miss Novak, you are in very dangerous territory. You and Mr. Naughton obviously seemed destined to wind up together at the end of the play.

PHYLLIS. Yes. That's the idea. Of course, the fun is in getting there. The audience expects it and actually looks forward to it.

JONATHAN. Yes, but you need to know that after the play ends, when you do begin going through life together...

PHYLLIS. Yes. What about it?

JONATHAN. Well, as I already told the audience, it's going to be a disaster. If there ever were two people so wrong for each other, it's you two. You're day and night.

PHYLLIS. Yes, I know that. But didn't you hear what I was just...

(Indicates audience)

...telling them? I'm going to change him. I'm going to make him into the perfect man for me. Yes, I'm sure we'll hit a few rough spots along the way, but I'm prepared for that. And as long as I control the ship, I'll make sure we avoid all rocks and reefs.

JONATHAN. Oh, boy. If there's anyone that needs to read my books, it's you. Miss Novak, try to understand this. In a good relationship there is no one in control, there is no one trying to change the other person. I'll tell you what. My books sell for twenty-five dollars each. Take all three, I'll let you have them for fifty-nine ninety-five tax included.

PHYLLIS. I'm sorry. I'm really not interested.

JONATHAN. Okay. How about all three for an even fifty? I'll also throw in an autographed picture.

PHYLLIS. It's not the price or your picture. I just feel I know what I'm doing and where I'm going with this situation and there's really no need for me to read any books.

JONATHAN. You're a very stubborn woman.

PHYLLIS. I like to think of myself as determined.

JONATHAN. I'm just trying to save you a lot of grief down the road. Look, do me a favor.

(Hands her a business card)

Take my card. Before this is over, chances are good you're going to need to seek professional help. I charge two-hundred and fifty an hour.

PHYLLIS. Two-fifty? I'd have to be crazy to pay that kind of money.

JONATHAN. Exactly.

(He EXITS. Phyllis looks at the card)

PHYLLIS. *(To audience)* Here's my problem with therapy. In today's world, I'm not so sure mental health is such a good thing?

(She sticks the card in her pocket)

All right. Back to business. First date with Bradley. Going to the movies.

(The lights darken. Phyllis is now in a pool of light. Bradley comes out pulling two stools. He now is in a grey sweater)

BRADLEY. I see you didn't change clothes.

PHYLLIS. I know. I see you didn't change colors.

(The two sit on the stools)

PHYLLIS *(CONTINUED)* *(Reminding audience)*
Okay. First date. Here we go.

(To Bradley)

How was your dinner?

BRADLEY. It was okay. I just wish I didn't let you talk me into the chicken. The roast beef looked great.

PHYLLIS. Red meat is a professional killer, Bradley. One day when you're in your nineties you'll thank me.

BRADLEY. When I'm in my nineties I can have soup. While I have teeth I'd like to have had the roast beef. What movie are we seeing?

PHYLLIS. I think something light. I don't want you to be any more upset than you are.

BRADLEY. I'm not upset.

PHYLLIS. You cried at the restaurant.

BRADLEY. Yes, but not until dessert. The dessert made me think of Joyce. She always ordered rice pudding.

PHYLLIS. You had apple pie.

BRADLEY. I know, but when they brought over the dessert tray the apple pie was right next to the rice pudding.

(Looks up at imaginary theatre marquee)

Oh, no.

PHYLLIS. Now what?

BRADLEY. This theatre. I used to come here all the time with Joyce.

PHYLLIS. You've got a long life ahead of you, Bradley. You're going to be going a lot of places that you and Joyce went to. Besides, what memories can a movie theatre have? You buy a ticket, you go in, you see a movie and you're done. Don't look for memories.

BRADLEY. You're right. You're absolutely right. That's what

I'll do. Screw memories. They're over. They're a thing of the past. You want some popcorn? I love popcorn. I always get popcorn.

PHYLLIS. No. Maybe just a box of Raisinettes.

BRADLEY. *(Bothered)* Raisinettes?

PHYLLIS. Yes, I like Raisinettes.

BRADLEY. Please don't order the Raisinettes.

PHYLLIS. I like Raisinettes.

BRADLEY. *(A pathetic plea)* Please don't order the Raisinettes. What if you had the red licorice instead? Maybe a box of Jordon Almonds?

PHYLLIS. Joyce ordered Raisinettes.

BRADLEY. She loved Raisinettes.

PHYLLIS. Everybody loves Raisinettes.

BRADLEY. Sometimes she'd have several boxes. I honestly don't know if I can stand to be around them. Not yet, anyway.

(Begins to sniffle)

PHYLLIS. Okay, okay! No crying. I'll have the red licorice.

BRADLEY. *(Getting hold of himself)* No. No it's not fair. If you want the Raisinettes have the Raisinettes. Why should you have to suffer because of Joyce and me?

PHYLLIS. Going without Raisinettes at the movies is not exactly something I d list as suffering.

BRADLEY. It doesn't matter. Now I insist you have the Raisinettes. People go to the movies, they eat Raisinettes. I need to deal with this like a grown up.

(Stretching his neck across an imaginary counter)

Miss, I'll have two boxes of Raisinettes please. One for my date and one for me.

(To Phyllis)

How was that?

PHYLLIS. Very brave. I'm impressed.

BRADLEY. Me too. I'm through being pushed around by Joyce's memories.

PHYLLIS. Good for you.

(To imaginary Clerk)

Oh, and Miss, I'll have a medium Coke.

BRADLEY. *(Sadly)* A Coke?

PHYLLIS. She liked Coke, too.

BRADLEY. She'd drink so much she sometimes had to go to the bathroom four times during one film.

PHYLLIS. *(To imaginary counter person)* Scratch the Coke.

BRADLEY. No. No, the hell with Joyce. She's in California with her old boyfriend. She's out of my life. She made that choice.

(Ordering)

And a large Coke, please.

PHYLLIS. I just wanted a medium.

BRADLEY. Raisinettes get you thirsty. I thought we could share the Coke.

PHYLLIS. But you don't like to share.

BRADLEY. I'd just be sharing with you, not the whole theatre. I can handle that. Do you mind if I get two straws. At least till we get to know each other's history a little better?

PHYLLIS. Fine. What about the popcorn?

BRADLEY. I don't know. I love popcorn, but I only have about fifty dollars in cash which barely covers the Raisinettes and Coke.

PHYLLIS. Get the popcorn. They take Master Card.

BRADLEY. *(Tortured)* They do? Damn! Damn! Damn!

PHYLLIS. *(A little fed up)* Now what?

BRADLEY. *(Starts to sniffle)* Joyce had a Master Card. Her last charges on it were for two plane tickets to California.

PHYLLIS. Oh, for Pete's sake. Let's go inside and see the movie.

BRADLEY. Right.

(They rise, take their stools and EXIT)

BLACKOUT

End Act I, Scene 3

Scene 4

TIME: A Saturday afternoon. One month later.

MITZI CARTRIGHT, *a woman in her mid to late 30's, walks around Phyllis's apartment, looking it over.*

MITZI. You know what this apartment needs? Adventure. Excitement. The way it is now, it's too perfect, too ordinary. Everything is where it's supposed to be. There's no mystery, no romance. You expect a chair there, there's a chair there. You expect a table there, there's a table there. The windows have drapes, the floor has a rug, the walls have pictures. Just what the hell is the statement? There is none. You know what I did to my living room? I said to hell with this everyday plebeian thinking. I threw caution to the wind. First I got rid of everything. Emptied the entire room. Then I had the walls painted chartreuse. For seating I scattered large fluffy pillows all around. Then in the center of the room I put in a large fish pond and filled it with a dozen or so large koi fish. With whatever space was left I filled it with plastic pink flamingos and large potted palms decorated with lights in motion. Well, now you walk into my living room and it's an explosion. People actually lose their balance when they first enter. My insurance company made me put in a hand rail near the front door. But I love what it's saying. "Here resides a woman dancing to her own music. A bold, daring woman. A trendsetter." Sure, a few people have thrown up when they first come in, but at least I know it stirred their imagination. I can't wait for you to come over and see it. Just be sure to bring some Dramamine.

(Phyllis ENTERS from kitchen with coffee)

PHYLLIS. I promise you, Mitzi, I will as soon as I find the time.

MITZI. Good. And wear boots. The goddamn koi fish slop water everywhere. So okay, doll, let's have it. I haven't heard from you in a month, how's it going? Is it working out, is it not working out?

PHYLLIS. With me and Bradley?

MITZI. Of course. I'm dying to know. You were going to mold him into the kind of guy that was right for you. It was a crazy scheme, but I say whatever gets the job done, go with it.

PHYLLIS. Well, it's been a little strange. It hasn't been the piece of cake I thought it would be.

MITZI. Of course not. Because the man is an absolute loser. I saw that right away.

PHYLLIS. That didn't seem to stop you from giving him your phone number at the Chinese restaurant.

MITZI. Honey, I give every man my phone number. It's a habit, not a validation. So, it's not working out?

PHYLLIS. Not the way I thought it would. I had very definite plans on how to fix him, reshape him, reconstruct him…

MITZI. Which is the only way a woman should go into a relationship.

PHYLLIS. It was clear from the very beginning we had nothing in common.

MITZI. Of course not. You're a rose garden. He's a manure pile.

PHYLLIS. Not books, not movies, not politics. Even our taste buds were different. I loved sushi. He hated sushi.

MITZI. I could never be with a man who hated sushi.

PHYLLIS. We root for different basketball teams.

MITZI. That's sick.

PHYLLIS. There was nothing we seemed to agree on.

MITZI. It had to be a living nightmare.

PHYLLIS. On our first date we had a terrible fight over who should pay for the cab.

MITZI. I knew he was cheap. I caught that right from the start, that sleazy little weasel.

PHYLLIS. I insisted on splitting it but no, no, not him.

MITZI. That penny pinching little twit.

PHYLLIS. He insisted on paying the whole thing.

MITZI. That money grubbing little...He did?

PHYLLIS. From then on all my plans went to hell. He stopped whining, he stopped complaining, he even stopped crying. He totally threw me off guard.

MITZI. That bastard.

PHYLLIS. That's just it. He wasn't. He turned out to be considerate, and kind, and sweet, traits I wasn't prepared for at all and slowly but surely I found I liked being with him just the way he was.

MITZI. You poor kid.

PHYLLIS. Look, don't get me wrong. He's not perfect by any means. Sometimes he can be a real pain in the ass. Sometimes he can be a bit insensitive. Sometimes he can be a bit obstinate. But you know what I realized? Sometimes I can too. The bottom line is that we both seem to be able to accept each other's imperfections. But most of all, and this is the biggest shocker of all, I really like being with him. And when I'm not, I actually miss him.

MITZI. I'm sick. I'm just sick about this.

PHYLLIS. Why?

MITZI. Because it happened to you and not me. And Bradley, does he feel the same way about you?

PHYLLIS. Well, he hasn't really said anything, but I have a sense that he does. At the start I just wanted to get his mind off his ex-wife, but after our first date her name never came up again. I think that's a very positive sign, don't you?

MITZI. Maybe. What about sex?

PHYLLIS. Well, no. Not yet.

MITZI. Hot and heavy petting?

PHYLLIS. No, not yet.

MITZI. French kissing?

PHYLLIS. No, not yet.

MITZI. Really? The whole thing sounds very perverted to me.

PHYLLIS. I set some pretty tough ground rules up front and he's been the perfect gentleman. Sometimes I really feel he'd like to make a move and now that I have these feelings for him, I wouldn't mind if he did, but he doesn't.

MITZI. I hate guys who won't take the initiative. I wonder if the bad experience with his wife could have turned him gay.

PHYLLIS. Can that happen?

MITZI. Oh, sure. It happened to two of my ex's after they left me.

PHYLLIS. It's so strange. I feel so comfortable with him, so at ease. Maybe it was because I felt so sure I was in control of the situation that I let my guard down. But I'm not going to even try to figure it out. All I know is that being with him gives me a wonderful feeling.

MITZI. So then what you're saying is, it's love?

PHYLLIS. You know I never used that word before, but I...I think it could be.

MITZI. And no sex?

PHYLLIS. That really doesn't seem important.

MITZI. Oh, please. Get real. If two people truly love each other there's sex. Even if only one person truly loves the other person, there can still can be sex. Of course, I found when neither person gives a damn about the other, that's when there's the best sex.

PHYLLIS. What's the point you're trying to make?

MITZI. No point. I'm just reminiscing. Anyway, since it seems like he's not going to make the first move, it's going to be up to you. Next time he comes over answer the door naked.

PHYLLIS. Oh, Mitzi, stop it.

MITZI. No, I'm serious. Just be sure it's him and not the building Super. That's happened to me once. On the plus side, I now know what the Super wants for Christmas.

(DOORBELL)

Expecting anyone?

PHYLLIS. No. Bradley's not coming over till this evening. We're going bowling.

(She opens the door. It's Bradley. He has a bouquet of flowers and a big smile on his face)

BRADLEY. Hi.

PHYLLIS. Hi. What a surprise. Come on in. You remember Mitzi.

BRADLEY. *(ENTERS room)* Yes. Of course. Uncle Wong Fu's.

MITZI. I'm still waiting for your call.

BRADLEY. Well, I uh…

MITZI. Please, no explanation necessary. I know the whole story. You got hung up on someone else. I understand perfectly.

BRADLEY. Well, I uh… .

MITZI. I saw it on your face the minute you walked in. It's so lit up, so alive. Can you see it Phyllis? I can see it. Something wonderful has happened to this man. Something recently has changed him from a pathetic, miserable, hopeless, the-whole-world-sucks kind of guy into a happy, glorious, thank-God-I'm-alive human being.

BRADLEY. *(Gloating)* It's that obvious, huh?

MITZI. Yes, and I'm sure once you have sex that smile will be twice as wide.

PHYLLIS. Come, on, Mitzi, you're embarrassing him.

MITZI. I'm simply telling it like it is, aren't I, Bradley? Something wonderful has happened to you, right?

BRADLEY. Well, there's no use keeping it inside any longer.

MITZI. Of course not.

BRADLEY. Something wonderful has happened to me.

MITZI. Out with it. Out with it. I'm dying to know what?

BRADLEY. Joyce is coming back to me.

MITZI. Great. *(And then reality sinks in)* What?

PHYLLIS. Joyce is…is…

BRADLEY. Coming back to me. And I owe it all to you, Phyllis. I owe it all to you.

(Stunned, the girls look at one another for a beat)

PHYLLIS & MITZI. Shit!

BLACKOUT

End of Act I

ACT II

Scene 1

TIME: Moments later. Phyllis and Mitzi are looking at Bradley, still stunned by the news of his going back to his ex-wife.

PHYLLIS. Joyce is coming back to you?

BRADLEY. Yes.

PHYLLIS. And you owe it all to me?

BRADLEY. Yes. You were right about everything. Getting involved with you took my mind off of her. I was so busy being with you, I stopped writing her, calling her. Naturally, she thought I found someone else, and I guess it made me more desirable. You know how some women think.

MITZI. Bradley, let me clue you in. No one in the entire universe knows how any woman thinks.

BRADLEY. Well, anyway, she called me last night, we got to talking and the end result is she's leaving her old boy-friend and coming back to me.

MITZI. And that's why you had that big smile on your face?

BRADLEY. Yes. It's like winning the lottery. One month ago there wasn't a prayer of her ever coming back to me. And now she can't wait to see me again. Who would have thought it possible?

MITZI. Not me.

BRADLEY. She's flying back next week. And Phyllis, I don't want you worrying about anything.

PHYLLIS. No?

BRADLEY. No. I know you need a guy like me in your life to help you with your commitment problem and I've got

43

just the one to take my place. His name is Jeffery. He works in my office and he's a bigger dork than I ever was. He's forty-two and still lives with his parents. Can you believe that? You date this guy for a month and even I might start looking good.

(Hands her the flowers)

Oh, these are for you. You'd better put them in water. I don't know why they're suddenly starting to wilt.

(Phyllis looks at him, takes the flowers, dumps them in a wastebasket and STORMS into the bedroom slamming the door behind her)

BRADLEY. *(CONTINUED)* What was that all about?

MITZI. You honestly haven't a clue.

BRADLEY. About what?

MITZI. Don't you get it, you bonehead? Phyllis is in love with you.

BRADLEY. In…in love…No she's not. She doesn't even like me.

MITZI. Now she doesn't. But a few seconds ago she loved you.

BRADLEY. She did? She loved me? Why? I'm not her type at all. She made that very clear. Besides, that wasn't part of the plan. I mean, it never entered my mind that she could possibly…I mean she's a very bright, beautiful woman who couldn't even bear the thought of having sex with me because well, even I have to admit I'm really nobody special.

MITZI. I know. Who would have guessed "nobody special" was her type.

BRADLEY. She's in love with me. I'm totally thrown.

MITZI. Unbelievable, isn't it?

BRADLEY. Gosh, I feel so awful about this. What do I do?

MITZI. What do you want to do?

BRADLEY. Well, I…I…I don't know.

MITZI. That's encouraging. Of course, what does it matter anyway? You're ex-wife is coming back to you, right?

BRADLEY. Yes. That's right. She is, isn't she?

MITZI. Is that a statement or a question?

BRADLEY. Please, don't confuse things any more than they are. Phyllis loves me? I don't get it.

MITZI. That makes two of us.

BRADLEY. I really need to think about this, don't I? The last thing I'd want to do is hurt her?

MITZI. Why?

BRADLEY. Because…Because she's my friend.

MITZI. And?

BRADLEY. And…And…

MITZI. Spit it out! Spit it out! Don't be afraid.

BRADLEY. And…and it's obvious that I…I…I

MITZI. Maybe jump to the next thought. We'll come back to the I, I, I…

BRADLEY. Look, tell Phyllis…tell Phyllis…

MITZI. Yes? What? What?

BRADLEY. Tell her…Tell her…I don't know what to tell her.

MITZI. Okay, I'll tell her.

BRADLEY. I'd better go. I need time to think.

MITZI. That's a good idea.

BRADLEY. See you.

MITZI. Sure. Oh, wait.

BRADLEY. *(At the door)* What?

MITZI. Before you go, that dork Jeffery you were talking about…

BRADLEY. Yes. What about him?

MITZI. Maybe you can give me his number.

(Bradley reacts)

BLACKOUT

End Act II, Scene 1

Scene 2

TIME: That evening.

Phyllis, on the sofa, is reading a book and sniveling, very similar to Bradley's sniveling in Act I. She speaks aloud to herself.

PHYLLIS. Why am I upset? I shouldn't be upset. He was nothing special. Nothing special's are a dime a dozen. He had a lot of hang ups. A lot of faults.

(She puts the book down and begins arguing with herself in two voices, one, upset, the other stern)

No, he didn't. – Yes, he did. – No, he didn't. – Yes, he did. – Okay, list some. – Well, he never argued with me. – Why should he? He wouldn't win anyway. – He never criticized me? – How could he? I'm perfect. – Well, maybe that's the problem. Once in awhile a couple could use a good spat to clear the air. – That's ridiculous. – No it isn't. – Yes it is and stop arguing with me. I'm not in the mood. – Oh, my. Aren't we bitchy today. – Look, I've had about enough from you. – Oh, yeah. Well, you started it.

(DOORBELL)

You want to get that because I'm not moving from here. – Fine.

(Phyllis goes to the door and opens it. It's Jonathan)

PHYLLIS *(CONTINUED)* Oh, you. What do you want now?

JONATHAN. I think you need someone to talk to.

PHYLLIS. Not really. I just had a wonderful conversation with myself.

(She heads for the sofa. Jonathan ENTERS the room, shuts the door)

JONATHAN. You probably need a little comfort and assurance.

PHYLLIS. About what?

JONATHAN. That in the long run, Bradley's going back to

his ex-wife is the best thing that can happen to you. Look, the one thing you've always been worried about is not being sure if a relationship will last. Well, I'm an expert in this field and believe me, with you and Bradley, there is no way.

PHYLLIS. Why do you keep saying that? I felt very comfortable with him. Very at ease. And every day it seemed to get better and better.

JONATHAN. How do you know you didn't talk yourself into it? This was a rescue operation for both of you from the beginning. You were two wounded birds trying to fly.

PHYLLIS. Well, apparently Bradley healed because he just flew the coop.

JONATHAN. Look, not to get off the issue, but between you and me, even if he was right for you, I think you could have picked someone with a little more going for him than Bradley. As far as I'm concerned, that guy is nothing special.

PHYLLIS. I keep hearing that. Which makes it even worse. If I can't hold on to someone who's nothing special, what does it say about me?

JONATHAN. I'm detecting low self esteem.

PHYLLIS. I never had it before.

JONATHAN. It's an acquired taste.

PHYLLIS. I believe I'm experiencing my first broken heart. Suddenly I want to eat a quart of ice cream.

JONATHAN. The heart is a very misleading organ and given much more respect than it deserves. Look at the track record it has. Dismal at best. Over half the marriages end in divorce, and about eighty percent of the rest of them aren't exactly jumping up and down with joy. This world is too romantic for it's own good. Do you know what the worst word ever invented in the world is?

PHYLLIS. Let me guess. Sauerkraut?

JONATHAN. Love!

PHYLLIS. Love? Why?

JONATHAN. Because it comes from here...

(Taps his chest)

...and not from here.

(Taps his head)

I'm telling you, you need to read my books. I don't know why I'm meeting such resistance. What if I let you have them for twelve-fifty each? That's my rock bottom price.

PHYLLIS. I don't want you to take this the wrong way, Doctor Alexander, but I am not interested in your books and I'm not interested in your advice. Maybe you need to go.

JONATHAN. Why, why, why do I always get involved with difficult people? Frankly, the only healthy one in this play is your friend Mitzi.

PHYLLIS. Oh, come on.

JONATHAN. No. I mean it. I love her attitude. When a relationship doesn't work she has the ability to move on. No moaning, no groaning. For someone in my line of work, that's so refreshing. After the play maybe I'll ask her to have a drink with me.

PHYLLIS. Good idea. And afterwards, if you need to talk to somebody, I charge three hundred an hour.

(PHONE RINGS)

Excuse me.

(Picks it up)

Yes.

(Downstage Left corner LIGHTS UP. Bradley is on a cordless phone)

BRADLEY. It's me, Bradley.

PHYLLIS. Hello, Bradley.

(She snivels throughout)

BRADLEY. Is it true, Phyllis? Do you love me?

PHYLLIS. Please, Bradley. It's not a good time for me to discuss this.

BRADLEY. *(Firmly)* Yes or no!

PHYLLIS. *(A louder snivel)* Yes.

BRADLEY. I'm so sorry. I had no idea.

PHYLLIS. Bradley, this is not your problem.

BRADLEY. Of course it is. You're my friend. My very good friend. When you have a problem, well, I have a problem.

PHYLLIS. Well, that seems to be the problem. I'm your good friend. But you seem to have become much more than that to me.

BRADLEY. I had no idea this was happening.

PHYLLIS. I know. But if you did, would it have mattered?

BRADLEY. Well, yes...uh, no...uh maybe. I don't know. I didn't let myself think about it. Don't forget, you really didn't like me. I was always aware of that, so I didn't let myself think past that point.

PHYLLIS. *(Almost under control)* I need to tell you something, Bradley. I wasn't playing fair with you. I had other motives, selfish motives. All along my intentions were to change you into a different person. Someone who would finally have all the attributes I was looking for and then I was going to keep you for myself.

BRADLEY. That was very ambitious.

PHYLLIS. Thank you.

BRADLEY. Well, the truth is, I wasn't playing fair with you either. Not really. I was so frightened of you, I was watching myself. I didn't want you to dislike me any more than you did the first day we met when we got our baggage mixed up. Do you remember what a complete jerk I was.

PHYLLIS. No.

BRADLEY. Well, try.

PHYLLIS. I don't want to.

BRADLEY. Look, I have a way to solve everything. Joyce isn't due back for a couple of days. Come out to dinner with me tonight.

PHYLLIS. What good would that do?

BRADLEY. You need to be reminded of what a loser I still am. Look, everything Joyce said about me in her letters was true. I'm boring, humorless, indifferent and cranky. That is the real me. I promise, you go to dinner with me tonight and I guarantee I'll be all those things again.

PHYLLIS. Bradley, that's what Joyce thought about you. I don't.

BRADLEY. Well, Joyce was right. All I ask is that you give me a chance to prove it. We'll go to Uncle Wong Fu's where we went the night we met. Remember, I moaned and complained so much, everyone was happy to see me leave. With no trouble at all I can still be that same idiot. I owe it to you.

PHYLLIS. That's very sweet of you, but I can't. I don't want to.

BRADLEY. No, don't argue with me. You're going to dinner with me and that's that. I'll be so detestable, I promise after tonight you'll never want to see me ever again. I'll pick you up in twenty minutes.

PHYLLIS. No. Please, Bradley…

BRADLEY. I'm leaving now.

PHYLLIS. No. No, don't pick me up. I'll…I'll meet you there.

BRADLEY. Promise?

PHYLLIS. I promise.

BRADLEY. Twenty minutes.

PHYLLIS. Yes. Twenty minutes.

BRADLEY. Good. I can't wait to see you.

(*They both hang up*)

BRADLEY. (*CONTINUED. Confused*) Why the hell did I say that?

(*The LIGHTS GO OUT on Bradley*)

PHYLLIS. *(To Jonathan)* He wants to see me.

JONATHAN. *(Upset)* Damn it. This play is going to end happily. I knew it, I knew it.

PHYLLIS. No it's not, because now I don't want it to. I've got him feeling sorry for me and that's not the way I want to trap a man. Oh, God. I just said "trap a man", didn't I?

JONATHAN. Yes you did and I can tell you exactly how it's going to happen. He'll be waiting for you in the restaurant. You'll be a little late giving him enough time to try and sort out his confused thoughts. And then in you walk, looking fabulous. A radiant angelic glow about you. A tear or two will be slowly moving down your cheek. A tear of love, a tear of passion. Both of you will do everything in your power to keep from rushing into each others arms.

PHYLLIS. I've got to be strong.

JONATHAN. The two of you are now sitting across from each other. He'll take your hand. "Look", he'll say, "no matter what happens, we will always be friends." And you'll say…

PHYLLIS. "No, we can't, Bradley. You can't be friends with someone you love. That always becomes a problem down the line. We've got to end it now."

JONATHAN. And he'll say, "We only live four blocks apart. We're bound to bump into each other now and then."

PHYLLIS. And I'll say, "We'll just ignore each other and go on. Besides you'll probably be with Joyce."

JONATHAN. And he'll say, "What if I'm not? Couldn't we even stop and make some small talk. Like, "Hi there. How are you doing?".

PHYLLIS. And I'll say, "No, we can't because what if I'm not doing well? It will be too painful"

JONATHAN. And he'll say, "Well, then lie because that's what I plan to do. And then the two of you will look into each others eyes. And then unable to control his true emotions any longer he'll scream out to the world…

PHYLLIS. "I love this woman, why don't I just admit it.

JONATHAN. And then you'll run into each others arms…

PHYLLIS. And hug and kiss and clutch…

JONATHAN. And he's dead meat. Shame on you.

PHYLLIS. *(She sits on the sofa)* That would be so wrong, so manipulative.

JONATHAN. Absolutely.

PHYLLIS. *(Lifting her knees to her chin and wrapping her arms around them in thought)*

On the other hand, if that's what a girl needs to do, then that's what a girl needs to do.

JONATHAN. I don't know why I'm wasting my time.

(The STAGE FADES TO BLACK as Jonathan walks to the front of the stage. His area LIGHTS UP and he addresses the audience once more)

JONATHAN *(CONTINUED)* Hello again. It's me. Doctor Jonathan Alexander. B.A., M.A., P.H.D. etcetera, etcetera. I know what's going through your mind. You're wondering why the hell doesn't he lay off those two people and let them work things out for themselves. Would you say that to a doctor who was treating someone for what could be a fatal illness? No. You'd want him to do everything in his power to save that person. That's his job. Well, my job is to save as many people as I can from being unhappy the rest of their lives. I remember how people scoffed when the phrase "preventative medicine" started coming into vogue. Imagine, trying to treat someone for a disease they don't yet have. Well, think of me as a forerunner of "preventative misery." If you can stop a disastrous union from happening before it happens, why not? And we do have the tools. Sometimes a simple little test will do it. Let me show you. By the way, this isn't part of the play, so don't let it throw you. I just need to prove a point so you'll understand my concern.

(Calls off)

Can you send those two out here for a minute.

(To audience)

By the way, all this is in my books which, incidentally, if your marriage is in trouble and you have a smart accountant, could be deductible.

(Phyllis, still in her robe and Bradley come out with their stools and sit on them)

PHYLLIS. You wanted us?

JONATHAN. Yes.

(Extending his hand to Bradley)

We've never met officially. I'm Jonathan Alexander. B.A. M.A PHD…

BRADLEY. *(skeptical)* Yeah, yeah, I've heard.

JONATHAN. I called you out here to perform a quick little test to prove to you and the audience that no matter how happily this play ends and no matter how much in love you are now, in the long run, the two of you are simply not compatible and the union will not work.

BRADLEY. Let me get this straight. You can tell whether our relationship will be successful or not with a test?

JONATHAN. Therapy has come along way.

BRADLEY. Screw therapy. The bottom line is that I like her and she likes me and we don't need any more of your negative interference.

PHYLLIS. You said "like," you didn't say "love."

BRADLEY. I'm obviously getting there. I'm sure once we meet at Uncle Wong Fu's and we hug, and kiss and clutch, those words will come out. Look, we're going to end up together, Phyllis, I just know it. But if it will make you feel better, we'll take the stupid test.

JONATHAN. Good for you. You won't be sorry.

BRADLEY. I wouldn't bet on that.

JONATHAN. Skeptics, skeptics, skeptics. It's amazing this world of ours makes any progress at all. Okay, now, the rules are very simple. When I give you a word, you give

me another word that comes immediately into your
heads.

PHYLLIS. Oh, you mean if you said black, I would say
white.

BRADLEY. And I would also say white.

JONATHAN. Exactly.

BRADLEY. That's such a hokey test. With all your carrying
on about how brilliant you are, I expected something
a little more complex.

JONATHAN. I promise you it will be. This is only the first
part to get you warmed up. Shall we begin?

PHYLLIS. Let's.

JONATHAN. Okay. Black!

PHYLLIS. White!

JONATHAN. Good.

BRADLEY. Wait a minute. Wait a minute. We already had
the answer to that one.

JONATHAN. Yes, I know. But when I give this test, I usually
start off with black. It was just a coincidence that Phyllis used that as an example. Besides, it doesn't matter.
There are no right or wrong answers. Now let's con-
tinue. Okay. Loose!

PHYLLIS. Tight!

BRADLEY. Yeah, tight.

JONATHAN. Light!

PHYLLIS. Dark!

BRADLEY. Yeah, dark.

JONATHAN. Big!

BRADLEY. Small!

(To Phyllis)

I beat you.

PHYLLIS. I don't think this is a competition.

BRADLEY. Oh. Well, maybe that's something you should
know about me. I can be competitive.

PHYLLIS. Really? I like a man that's competitive.

JONATHAN. No, you don't.

PHYLLIS. Yes, I do.

JONATHAN. No, you don't.

BRADLEY. Hey, if she says she does, she does.

PHYLLIS. Oh, Bradley, that's so nice of you to stick up for me.

BRADLEY. I'm also very protective.

PHYLLIS. I adore a man that's protective.

BRADLEY. Yeah? So far I think I'm doing pretty good with this test.

JONATHAN. That was not part of the test.

PHYLLIS. *(Reaching out and taking Bradley's hand)* Too bad. I really like his answers.

JONATHAN. Can we go on?

BRADLEY. Be our guest.

JONATHAN. Happy!

PHYLLIS. Sad!

BRADLEY. I promise I'll never make you sad, Phyllis.

PHYLLIS. I believe you, Bradley.

JONATHAN. Will you just respond without any commentary, please? You really are a pain in the ass, Bradley. No wonder your wife left you.

PHYLLIS. Excuse me, Doctor Alexander but that was a very unkind thing to say.

JONATHAN. No, it wasn't.

PHYLLIS. Yes, it was.

JONATHAN. Can we please get on with the test and not be so argumentative?

BRADLEY. She is not argumentative.

JONATHAN. Yes, she is.

BRADLEY. No, she isn't.

JONATHAN. Yes, she is and I'm the professional here. Now goddamn it, let's get back to the test.

BRADLEY. Okay. She said sad, I said sad.

JONATHAN. Good. Very good. Potato!

PHYLLIS. Tomato!

BRADLEY. Pancakes!

PHYLLIS. Pancakes?

BRADLEY. Yeah, pancakes.

JONATHAN. That's very interesting. I never got that response to potato ever.

BRADLEY. I guess in my own way, I'm a very unique person.

PHYLLIS. I revere unique people.

BRADLEY. I sensed it.

JONATHAN. Unique? I don't think so. Strange, troubled. That's more like it. We need to explore that pancake answer a little more.

BRADLEY. I thought there were no right or wrong answers in this test.

JONATHAN. There aren't. But there *are* disturbing answers.

BRADLEY. Oh, get off it. I said pancakes because that's what came to mind when you said potato. Potatoes make me think of pancakes. My mother made great potato pancakes. I don't see what the problem is.

JONATHAN. Well, the normal expected response to potato is tomato, as Phyllis responded. But pancakes, well, I'm afraid when something of this magnitude appears so early in the test it does not bode well for the two of you.

PHYLLIS. Maybe if you gave him the word in the reverse sequence that might have made a difference. Maybe if you started with tomato maybe then he would have said potato.

BRADLEY. Yes. That's a possibility. When you started with potato I really had only one way to go. That was pancakes.

JONATHAN. Well, okay, it's worth a try. Let's start with tomato.

BRADLEY. Soup!

PHYLLIS. Soup?

BRADLEY. Tomato soup. I love to have it with potato pancakes. Tomato soup and potato pancakes, they're my favorite. Together it's an unbeatable combination.

JONATHAN. You are not cooperating. This is just another reason why I think this relationship is headed for the crapper. You're a very confused person, Bradley. If you're having difficulty with these simple choices, God only knows what's ahead. But compatibility is a definite issue.

BRADLEY. I'm just being responsive. Isn't that what you wanted? So far it looks like the only one I'm not compatible with is you and that suits me fine. Let's just get on with it, okay?

JONATHAN. No!

BRADLEY. Why not?

JONATHAN. Because you're an imbecile.

BRADLEY. I am not!

JONATHAN. You are too!

BRADLEY. Am not!

JONATHAN. Are too!

BRADLEY. Take that back.

JONATHAN. Will not!

BRADLEY. Will too!

JONATHAN. Jerk!

BRADLEY. Creep!

JONATHAN. Dope!

BRADLEY. Moron!

JONATHAN. Nitwit.

BRADLEY. Lame brain!

JONATHAN. Idiot!

BRADLEY. Cretin!

PHYLLIS. *(Trying to stop them)* Guys!

BRADLEY & JONATHAN. Girls!

JONATHAN. Dick head!

BRADLEY. Ass face!

PHYLLIS. Stop!

BRADLEY & JONATHAN. *(Facing each other angrily)* Go!

PHYLLIS. Enough!

BRADLEY & JONATHAN. More!

PHYLLIS. *(In desperation)* Potato!

BRADLEY & JONATHAN. Pancakes!

> *(Bradley and Jonathan look at one another in confusion and then scream)*

> *BLACKOUT*

End Act II, Scene 2

Scene 3

TIME: Later that same evening. Phyllis, alone, in her robe and in deep thought, sits on the sofa as she was earlier in the last scene, her arms wrapped around her knees and her chin resting on them.

(DOORBELL)

Hesitantly, she rises, crosses to the door and opens it. It's Bradley. He ENTERS and closes the door behind him.

BRADLEY. You stood me up.

PHYLLIS. I know.

BRADLEY. I kept calling.

PHYLLIS. I couldn't pick up the phone.

BRADLEY. I waited in that restaurant over two hours.

PHYLLIS. I'm sorry.

BRADLEY. I had four orders of Kung Pao Chicken.

PHYLLIS. I hope you liked it.

BRADLEY. You would have been proud of me. I gave every one in the restaurant a taste. I hope I won't catch something. They all used my fork. Why didn't you come?

PHYLLIS. I wanted to. I couldn't. I couldn't move. Bradley, I've been giving our situation a lot of thought. You need to go back to Joyce.

BRADLEY. Why?

PHYLLIS. Because I kept thinking how happy you were at the thought of her returning.

BRADLEY. I know. But at the restaurant I realized it was really a vindictive happy. The joy I was experiencing came from a spiteful sense of revenge. Besides, getting back together was really Joyce's idea, not mine. And I'm not so sure it would work out any better this time. You told me, you weren't able to change me. I'm afraid even if she came back she'd soon be disappointed again. I could never be who she wants me to be. Besides, her college reunion is next month. Who knows who she'll meet there.

PHYLLIS. But you had feelings for her. Remember how broken up you were when you came back from California? You loved her.

BRADLEY. No. I thought about that at the restaurant too. I was in love with marriage, not Joyce. I was in love with having someone in my life. When she left, sure there was an emptiness. But if you really love someone, there's no way you can forget them in a week, or a month, the way I did when you came into my life. Look, if Joyce never left me, maybe we would have hung in and made it together. But she did leave and that changed everything. I discovered something very important. It wasn't so much that I didn't have a wife. It was that I realized I didn't have a friend. You are my friend, Phyllis. And for me, that's what it's all about. Today, you told me you loved me. I thought about that a lot. And I liked that you loved me. I liked it very much. And once I gave myself permission to think about us going a little further than friendship, I realized I love you too.

PHYLLIS. We are desperate people, Bradley. It's very possible we could have talked ourselves into this relationship.

BRADLEY. What does it matter how we got here? The only thing that matters is that we got here and we want to be here.

PHYLLIS. I know. It's just that now I'm not sure if that's enough.

(DOORBELL)

Who could that be this late?

(Phyllis opens the door. It's Mitzi and Jonathan. Mitzi is carrying three books)

MITZI. Surprise!

(She ENTERS with Jonathan behind her)

(Indicating Jonathan) This is Doctor Jonathan Alexander, a professional, licensed psychologist with degrees from several prestigious Universities.

PHYLLIS. A B.A, an M.A, a P.H.D. Yes, yes. We know all that.

MITZI. We met in the theatre lobby. See these three books. They're his. They're originally twenty-five dollars apiece. He let me have all three for thirty bucks and for an extra five dollars he personally autographed them.

BRADLEY. Too bad. Now you can't return them to a bookstore.

JONATHAN. Best part's coming up.

MITZI. After I bought the books he asked me out for a drink. You'll never guess what happened then.

BRADLEY. You went to a motel.

MITZI. Better. We started talking and discovered we have very close ties to each other. He treated all three of my ex-husbands.

BRADLEY. Before you married them or after?

MITZI. After, of course. They were perfectly healthy before I married them. Anyway, Doctor Alexander and I talked and talked and talked the whole evening and guess what happened?

BRADLEY. He got a headache.

JONATHAN. Much worse. I lost my heart to this woman.

PHYLLIS. So fast?

JONATHAN. When it comes to love the boundaries of time are transparent at best.

MITZI. I just adore the way college educated guys talk. They're really quite smart. Anyway, then he did something to me, no man has ever done before…He gave me a test.

BRADLEY. Smart move. In today's world you never know where anyone's been.

MITZI. Not that kind of test. A more involved one. To see if we were compatible. He would say a word and I would answer with whatever popped into my head. Like he said…

(Points at Jonathan)

JONATHAN. Day!

MITZI. And I said, "Doorbell!

PHYLLIS. *(Sarcastic)* Totally logical.

MITZI. He said…

(Points at Jonathan)

JONATHAN. Dog!

MITZI. And I said, "Butterfly net!".

BRADLEY. I think we can use two right now.

MITZI. Then the craziest thing happened. He said…

(Points at Jonathan)

JONATHAN. Potato.

PHYLLIS. And you said…?

MITZI. "Pancakes!"

BRADLEY. Isn't it a small world?

PHYLLIS. And then?

MITZI. And then he had what looked like a seizure. He threw himself on the floor and began kicking his feet and ranting and raving. I had to call the paramedics.

PHYLLIS. Oh, my.

MITZI. That's just what I said.

JONATHAN. Fortunately, it was just an anxiety attack.

MITZI. At first I thought it was from the thrill of meeting me.

JONATHAN. That was part of it. The other part was that I suddenly realized that for some unexplained reason, I was absolutely mad for this woman, no matter how warped she was. And if there were any two people more wrong for each other, it was us.

BRADLEY. Yes, but you two would be wrong for anybody.

JONATHAN. Well, that's just it. After the paramedics calmed me down…

MITZI. I had to sit on his chest.

JONATHAN. I knew I had to come back here as quickly as I could.

PHYLLIS. The reason being…

JONATHAN. Because in my one brief encounter with Mitzi, I came to the realization that there is no greater power or sensation in the world than being in love. And so I felt it was my duty as a professional, licensed psychologist…

MITZI. With degrees from several prestigious universities…

JONATHAN. …to tell you that…

BRADLEY. You were full of crap.

JONATHAN. Yes, exactly. And all the rules, all the common sense, all the red warning flags that I've been writing about are meaningless, because once you've experienced love, as I have for this fabulous woman…

(Hugs Mitzi around the waist)

You'd have to be nuts to run away from it

MITZI. Did I get lucky or did I get lucky?

JONATHAN. So keeping that in mind, my next move has to be this.

(He takes the books from Mitzi)

Don't worry about these books, Sweetie. I promise I'll give you a full refund.

(He dumps them in the waste basket)

PHYLLIS. Whoa! That had to hurt.

JONATHAN. Basically, what I'm telling you two now is go ahead, fall in love and end this play how ever you want. Love turns us all into helpless ninnies anyway, so don't fight it. And more importantly, enjoy every minute of it you can, because who knows if it will ever come your way again?

MITZI. I am very fortunate. This is the fourth time for me.

JONATHAN. Well, good luck to both of you. I know you'll do the right thing.

(To Mitzi)

Come on, Honey.

MITZI. Where to?

JONATHAN. A deli. Suddenly I have a taste for tomato soup and potato pancakes.

(They EXIT. A beat)

BRADLEY. I'm not quite sure what that was all about?

PHYLLIS. It was about two screwed up people who for some mysterious reason are absolutely perfect for each other.

BRADLEY. That's *our* story.

PHYLLIS. A little frightening isn't it?

BRADLEY. No, a little magical. I'm not saying our being together is going to be a cake walk. We all come with baggage. But together maybe we can help each other unpack. Who knows how anything ends up? All I know for sure is that at this particular moment, I want to be with you for the rest of my life and I'm not going to let you get away from me.

PHYLLIS. That's so romantic.

BRADLEY. I know and I didn't even know I could be romantic.

PHYLLIS. So now what?

BRADLEY. How's this?

(He takes her in his arms and they kiss)

PHYLLIS. Nice. Very nice.

BRADLEY. I love you, Phyllis Novak.

PHYLLIS. And I love you Bradley Naughton. It's a wonderful start isn't it?

BRADLEY. Yes. And not a bad ending either.

(They kiss again)

LIGHTS FADE

THE END

PROPS

ACT I

Scene 1
Large, wheeled suitcase with telescopic handle packed with various articles of men's clothing
An identical suitcase with telescopic handle not working
Can of diet root beer
Small suitcase lock
12 various size envelopes tied with a red ribbon
Box of Kleenex
Purse

Scene 3
Glass of milk
Man's wallet
3 wallet sized photos
Business card for Jonathan
Two stools

Scene 4
A tray with two cups of coffee
Bouquet of flowers

ACT II

Scene 2
Book
Cordless phone for Bradley
2 stools

Scene 3
3 books

COSTUMES

ACT I

Scene 1
Phyllis – Slacks and sweater
Bradley - Grey jacket, grey slacks, grey shirt

Scene 2
Jonathan – Blue blazer, dark slacks, white shirt, blue tie.
His outfit remains the same throughout play.

Scene 3
Phyllis same as Scene 1
Bradley same as Scene 1, later a grey sweater instead of jacket.

Scene 4
Mitzi – Dress
Phyllis – Dress
Bradley – V neck sweater, shirt and slacks

ACT II

Scene 1
All in same outfits as in Act I, Scene 4.

Scene 2
Phyllis – Attractive bathrobe
Bradley – Same as in Act I, Scene 4

Scene 3
Phyllis – Same as previous scene
Bradley – Sport coat, slacks, shirt
Mitzi – A different dress

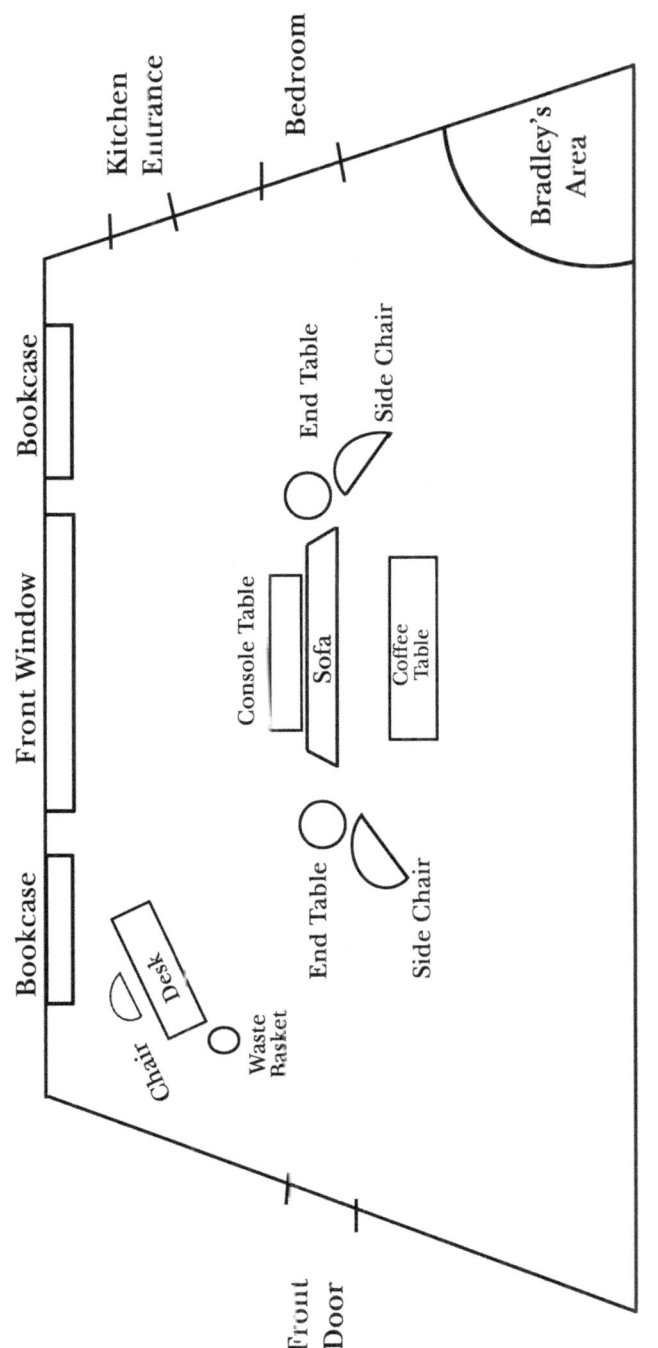

SET PLOT

Also by
Sam Bobrick...

Annoyance
Are You Sure?
The Crazy Time
Death in England
Flemming (An American Thriller)
Getting Sara Married
Hamlet II (Better Than the Original)
Last Chance Romance
Murder at the Howard Johnson's
New York Water
No Hard Feelings
Norman, Is That You?
The Outrageous Adventures of
Sheldon and Mrs. Levine
Passengers
Remember Me?
Splitting Issues
The Stanway Case
Wally's Cafe
Weekend Comedy

OTHER TITLES AVAILABLE FROM SAMUEL FRENCH

JACK GOES BOATING
Bob Glaudini

Full Length / Comedy / 2m, 2f / Interior
Four flawed but likeable lower-middle-class New Yorkers interact in a touching and warmhearted play about learning how to stay afloat in the deep water of day-to-day living. Laced with cooking classes, swimming lessons and a smorgasbord of illegal drugs, *Jack Goes Boating* is a story of date panic, marital meltdown, betrayal, and the prevailing grace of the human spirit.

"An immensely likable play [that] exudes a wry compassion."
- *The New York Times*

"Endearing romantic comedy about a married couple and the social-misfit friends they fix up. Witty and knowing and all heart."
- *Variety*

"Glides effortlessly from the shallow end of the emotional pool to the deep end."
- *Theatremania.com*

OTHER TITLES AVAILABLE FROM SAMUEL FRENCH

ELECTION DAY
Josh Tobiessen

Full Length / Comedy / 2m, 2f / Unit Set
It's Election Day, and Adam knows his over-zealous girlfriend will never forgive him if he fails to vote. But when his sex starved sister, an eco-terrorist, and a mayoral candidate willing to do anything for a vote all show up, Adam finds that making that quick trip to the polls might be harder than he thought. *Election Day* is a hilarious dark comedy about the price of political (and personal) campaigns.

"An outrageous comedy… at double-espresso speed."
- The New York Times

"Ridiculously entertaining… cute and cutting."
- Variety

"Laugh-out-loud."
- Backstage

"Delightfully farcical… Tobiessen takes a simple premise and spins it out into a hilarious sequence of events. His dialogue is lean and playful, and includes some terrific lines."
- Theatermania

OTHER TITLES AVAILABLE FROM SAMUEL FRENCH

BACH AT LEIPZIG
Itamar Moses

Comedy Farce / 7m / Interior

Leipzig, Germany — 1722. Johann Kuhnau, revered organist of the Thomaskirche, suddenly dies, leaving his post vacant. The town council invites musicians from across to audition for the coveted position, among them young Johann Sebastian Bach. In an age where musicians depend on patronage from the nobility or the church to pursue their craft, the post at a prominent church in a cultured city is a near guarantee of fame and fortune – which is why some of the candidates are willing to resort to any lengths to secure it. *Bach at Leipzig* is a fugue-like farcical web of bribery, blackmail, and betrayal set against the backdrop of Enlightenment questions about humanity, God, and art.